WHAT'S THE MATTER, AUNTY MAY?

by Peter Friend   illustrated by Andrew Joyner

I have some questions, Aunty May.
Why *did* you shout at me today?
And why were you a little gruff?
Why did you scream, 'Enough! Enough!'

Was it because I tried to help –
was *that* why you began to yelp?
When I began to sweep the floor . . .

and knocked the broom
through your screen door?

Or was it when
I tried to clean
your antique vase,
which fell between

the cupboard and the lounge-room wall
and now is not a vase at all?

At least I cleaned up all the bits
and now it much more neatly fits

beside that precious antique cup
that somehow slipped when I washed up.

Or are you sad
about your cat,
whom you left snoozing
on the mat?
I only tripped
and spilt red ink,

but red ink fades quite soon to pink!

Perhaps your budgie made you sad?
But she'll recover. Don't get mad.

She's just (I guess) a little meaner
since passing through the vacuum cleaner.

I tried to dust
your bookshelves, too.
Could *that* have been
what bothered you?

I had to climb
because I'm short.
They weren't as strong
as I had thought.

Or was it, Aunty, when I tried
to fix your bathroom sink, inside –
and then I heard that funny thud
that burst your pipes and caused that flood?

The lounge room looked just like a lake.
I served you up that HUGE cream cake,
or would have if I hadn't hit . . .

the ceiling fan and splattered it.

Yes, everywhere and round about
are signs that I have helped you out,
so why are you so filled with gloom
when you survey each finished room?

Why aren't you happy, Aunty May,
that someone helped you clean today?

Little Hare Books
an imprint of
Hardie Grant Egmont
Ground Floor, Building 1, 658 Church Street
Richmond, VIC 3121, Australia

www.littleharebooks.com

First published 2012
First published in paperback 2012

A version of this text was first published in *The School Magazine*,
NSW Department of Education and Communities, 2009

Cataloguing-in-Publication details are available from the
National Library of Australia

978-1-921894-12-1 (pbk.)

Designed by Vida & Luke Kelly
Produced by Pica Digital, Singapore
Printed through Phoenix Offset
Printed in Shen Zhen, Guangdong Province, China,
December 2011

5 4 3 2 1

For Mum and Dad and my family—PF
For Laurence and Marigold—AJ